CORDUROY Makes a Cake

A Viking Easy-to-Read

Story by **Alison Inches**

Illustrations by **Allan Eitzen**

Based on the characters created by
Don Freeman

VIKING

VIKING
Published by the Penguin Group
Penguin Putnam Books for Young Readers,
345 Hudson Street, New York, New York 10014, U.S.A.
Penguin Books Ltd, 27 Wrights Lane, London W8 5TZ, England
Penguin Books Australia Ltd, Ringwood, Victoria, Australia
Penguin Books Canada Ltd, 10 Alcorn Avenue, Toronto, Ontario, Canada M4V 3B2
Penguin Books (N.Z.) Ltd, 182-190 Wairau Road, Auckland 10, New Zealand

Penguin Books Ltd, Registered Offices: Harmondsworth, Middlesex, England

First published in 2001 by Viking,
a division of Penguin Putnam Books for Young Readers.

1 3 5 7 9 10 8 6 4 2

Copyright © Penguin Putnam Inc., 2001
Text by Alison Inches
Illustrations by Allan Eitzen
All rights reserved

LIBRARY OF CONGRESS CATALOGING-IN-PUBLICATION DATA
Inches, Alison.
Corduroy makes a cake / based on characters created by Don Freeman ;
by Alison Inches ; illustrated by Allan Eitzen.
p.   cm.
Summary: Corduroy sets out to make Lisa a special surprise for her birthday
but it turns out to be much harder than it looks.
ISBN 0-670-88946-6 (hardcover)
[1. Teddy bears—Fiction. 2. Birthday cakes—Fiction.
3. Birthdays—Fiction. 4. Cake—Fiction.] I. Freeman, Don. II. Eitzen,
Allan, ill. III. Title.
PZ7.I355 Cm 2001
[E]—dc21
2001000511

Viking ® and Easy-to-Read ® are registered trademarks of Penguin Putnam Inc.

Printed in Singapore
Set in Bookman

Reading Level 1.9

CORDUROY Makes a Cake

Lisa slipped on her backpack.

"Today is my birthday," she said.

"I'm having a party!"

Lisa gave Corduroy a hug.

Then she left for school.

A birthday party? thought Corduroy.

I love birthday parties.

I will make Lisa a Corduroy Cake!

Corduroy put on an apron

and a cook's hat.

He got everything he needed:

1 cake mix

2 cake pans

2 cans of pink frosting

1 bowl

2 eggs

1 cup of water

And one thing he did not need.

Crash!

A bag of flour.

Corduroy dusted himself off.

Then, **r-r-r-rip!**

He opened the cake mix

and dumped it into the bowl.

Crack! Plop! Splash!

He added the eggs and water.

Then he turned on the mixer.

Low: **Whirrrrr.**

Medium: **Whirrrr.**

Full blast: **WHIRRRR!**

The batter hit the walls.

It hit the floor.

It hit Corduroy.

"This is fun!" said Corduroy.

Then he put the batter into the pans.

But there was not enough batter.

"Oh, dear," said Corduroy.

"I need more cake mix."

He looked high

and low.

But there was no more cake mix.

Then he saw a box on the counter.

He opened it

and looked inside.

"A cake!" said Corduroy.

"Now I don't need to make one."

But the cake had nothing on it.

"It needs words," said Corduroy.

He opened the pink frosting

and put it into a bag.

"I can write on it," he said.

"But first I need practice."

He took the frosting to the bathroom.

He practiced on the tub.

He practiced on the counter.

He even practiced on the mirror.

"Wow!" said Corduroy.

"Now I am good!"

Then, **Click!**

He heard a key in the door.

"Uh-oh," said Corduroy.

"Somebody's coming!"

He ran into the sewing room.

He shut the door

and hid under a shelf.

Clunk!

A round box landed on Corduroy's head.

Then he heard a voice in the kitchen.

"My goodness!" cried the voice.

"What a mess!"

Lisa's mother! thought Corduroy.

He listened to her feet.

Click, click, click.

They walked one way.

Click, click, click.

They walked the other way.

Sweep!

Bang!

Clank!

Corduroy listened some more.

The feet ran upstairs

and into the bathroom.

He heard a shout.

The feet ran downstairs.

Corduroy came out from under the boxes.

He felt terrible.

He had not made a cake for Lisa.

He had just made a mess.

But then Corduroy had an idea.

He picked up a pink button.

Neat!

And a green button.

Cool!

And another!

And another!

Corduroy got some glue

and got to work.

Soon he forgot about the cake

and the mess.

He even forgot he felt terrible until . . .

Click! Click! Click!

Lisa's mother!

Corduroy hid inside the box.

Creak!

The door opened.

"What's this?" said her mother.

"It must be for Lisa!"

She picked up the box with

Corduroy and took him away.

Then she put the box on a table.

Corduroy heard things from inside the box.

He heard the doorbell.

Ding! Dong!

Ding! Dong!

He heard children's voices.

He heard laughter and horns.

Then he heard a voice say,

"Where's Corduroy?"

It was Lisa.

"Corduroy will turn up," said her mother.

"It's time for presents."

"Yes!" cried her friends.

"Open your presents!"

So Lisa did.

She opened a big present.

"A tea set!" said Lisa.

She opened a little present.

"A necklace!" she said.

Then she picked up the box with Corduroy.

"This box looks like a cake!" said Lisa.

She shook the box.

Corduroy went up and down.

She shook it again.

Corduroy went from side to side.

Then Lisa took off the lid and looked inside.

"Corduroy!" she cried.

Lisa picked Corduroy up.

She held him close.

"I love my Corduroy cake!" said Lisa.

Corduroy felt very proud.

Happy birthday, Lisa! he thought.

"Happy birthday!" said her friends.

Everyone blew party horns.

Then they shouted,

"Hooray for Lisa!

Hooray for Corduroy!"

And hooray for my Corduroy Cake!

thought Corduroy.